The Grumpy Bunny's®
Too Many Bunnybabies

W9-BME-351

by Justine Korman • illustrated by Lucinda McQueen

*For my parents, Marvin & Eleanore, who read to me.
In the fond hope that they'll someday read to their grandchildren.
—J.K.*

*For Roy, always a true gentleman and a wonderful person to work with!
Warm regards and many thanks.
—L.M.*

As soon as school was done for the day, Hopper the grumpy bunny hurried to see his favorite friend, Lilac, who was the music teacher. But she was on her way out. "I'm going to read at the Bunnybaby Center's storytime," Lilac explained.

"How can you read to babies?" Hopper grumbled. "They don't understand you!"

"Bunnybabies love stories!" Lilac said. "And reading to babies now makes them good readers when they grow up."

"Why don't you come in and see?" Lilac suggested.
So Hopper followed her into the Easter Bunny Elementary School's Bunnybaby Center.

Lilac introduced Hopper to Mrs. Milkweed, who took care of the bunnybabies.

Mrs. Milkweed soon had all the little ones settled in a circle on the floor, and Lilac began to read them a story.

But before she could finish the first book, the music teacher got a phone call.

"My sister is having her babies! I've got to go to the hospital!" she exclaimed.

Lilac turned to Hopper. "Can you take over?"

Hopper wasn't so sure about finishing Lilac's storytime. But Mrs. Milkweed had her paws full, and no one else was around to help.

Reluctantly Hopper started reading.
But the bunnybabies had other ideas. . . .

Dandylion threw a book!

Flora took off her diaper and waved it like a flag!

Alfalfa ate a page!

"Oh, nettles and burrs!" Mrs. Milkweed exclaimed.
"The wee ones always get a bit fussy before their nap."
A bit fussy?! Hopper thought. This was chaos!
The bunnybabies had gotten into the books and
toys—and they were out of control!

"They're great little readers once they get settled,"
Mrs. Milkweed assured Hopper. "Could you help, please?"

As Hopper looked around at the bunnybabies, his first thought was to hop away as fast as his feet would take him. But then he remembered Lilac and knew she was counting on him.

So while Mrs. Milkweed fed Alfalfa, Hopper tried to keep Dandylion off the bookshelf and get Flora into a clean diaper.

Unfortunately, Flora wasn't the only bunnybaby
who needed a new diaper. "Grrr-oss!" Hopper grumbled.

Finally, all the bunnybabies were settled back in their circle.

Once again, Hopper began to read—and this time the bunnybabies listened.

They giggled when Hopper used funny voices.

They looked at the pictures.

They even seemed to understand!

After three stories, Mrs. Milkweed handed Hopper a bedtime book. "They love to hear this one before their nap," she explained.

Hopper read the gentle bedtime tale and . . .

. . . dozed off himself! Soon he was having an amazing dream.
He saw books and bunnybabies . . . bunnybabies and books. . . .

Suddenly Lilac appeared in Hopper's dream. "Hopper,"
she said, "I'm an aunt! I'm an aunt six times over!"
    "You can't be an ant. You're a bunny," Hopper grumbled.

When he heard Lilac giggle, the grumpy bunny woke up.
Lilac looked admiringly at the happy, comfortable
bunnybabies. "And since you're so good with little ones,
I'm sure you'll want to help with the babysitting," she said.

Me? Good with bunnybabies? Hopper thought.
Then he grinned. Maybe he was! And despite the diapers, Hopper had to admit that the little ones were lots of fun!

"Sure, I'll babysit," he agreed.

That's when Hopper had a truly scary thought. Maybe someday he would even have bunnybabies of his own!

All bunnybabies need these things:
Clean diapers, milk, and toys.
But books are also something great
for little girls and boys!

The Grumpy
Easter Bunny

by Justine Korman • illustrated by Lucinda McQueen

For Ron, the grumpiest bunny of all
—J.K.

For Alex Guitar
—Lots of love from Aunt Lucy

Deep in the forest on
the night before Easter, the bunnies
danced under the moon. They were all as
happy as . . . well, Easter bunnies—except for one
grumpy bunny named Hopper.

After the bunnies had finished dancing, Sir Byron, the Great Hare, told them, "You are the messengers of spring. Go now, and spread love and joy!"

Hopper kicked a stone and grumbled, "Joy and love. Ha! I hate that mushy stuff."

As he waited in line for his wheelbarrow full of
Easter treats, Hopper grew even grumpier. What was the
point of making treats all year and then running your
paws off to hide them for someone else to find?

While the other bunnies gladly began their rounds, Hopper dragged his already tired feet.

Hopper gazed at the heap of chocolate bunnies, marshmallow chicks, caramels, raspberry creams, and other delights.

"I wish all these treats were mine," he thought hungrily.

Then his ears flew up with a wicked idea.
"They could be mine!" he said. "Who will ever
know if I keep the goodies or give them away?"
Hopper ran to his burrow, pushing the heavy
wheelbarrow as fast as he could.

Hopper tried to roll the heavy wheelbarrow inside, but it was too wide. He pushed and shoved and pushed some more.

He was so busy pushing, Hopper didn't notice a strawberry-cream-filled egg fall off the wheelbarrow. The egg rolled down the shady path toward the stream.

Hopper puffed up his tiny chest. Then he pushed with all his might. The wheelbarrow lurched forward, and the grumpy bunny fell flat on his face.

"That was almost as hard as delivering the treats," Hopper complained.

But at last, the goodies were inside. Hopper ran
his paws through the mountains of candy. He juggled
jellybeans and made marshmallow nests for the
chocolate eggs.

Then he began to eat.

And eat.

And eat!

Hopper gobbled and gnawed the whole night through. Now he didn't feel so grumpy, but he did feel very sticky and a little too full.

Finally he decided to go to the stream to get a nice, cool drink.

Hopper stopped when he heard a *mew, mew, mew*. He peeked out from behind a tree and saw Lottie, Spottie, and Dottie, three kittens who lived nearby.

Hopper hid in the
reeds and listened.
"They must be here
somewhere," Spottie mewed.
"This *is* Easter morning,
isn't it?" Lottie asked.
"Oh, dear," Hopper thought. "The kittens are searching
for Easter treats—and they aren't going to find any!"
Hopper felt an uncomfortable stirring deep
inside. Should he have eaten the treats? Had he
done the wrong thing?

Then, to Hopper's great surprise, Dottie cried, "I found one!"

She had found the strawberry-cream-filled egg that had fallen off his wheelbarrow.

Before Hopper could say a word, Spottie and Lottie rushed to their sister.

"I'm the oldest," Spottie said, grabbing for the egg.

"I'm the hungriest," Lottie argued.

"I found it!" Dottie squeaked.

Hopper felt terrible as
he watched the kittens wrestle
and hiss in the dewy grass.
    Suddenly, the kittens rolled right
over the egg and smashed it to bits. They
stopped wrestling and stared at the gooey mess.

"We should have shared," Spottie mewed sadly.
"We shouldn't have been greedy," Lottie sighed.
"We'll divide what's left of it," Dottie said firmly.
Then the three kittens hugged.

"Oh, dear," Hopper said to himself. He turned away from the kittens—only to find himself nose-to-nose with Sir Byron, the Great Hare!

"Why haven't you delivered to your area?" Sir Byron demanded.

Hopper opened his mouth, but no sound came out. The chocolate that was smeared all over his face said it all.

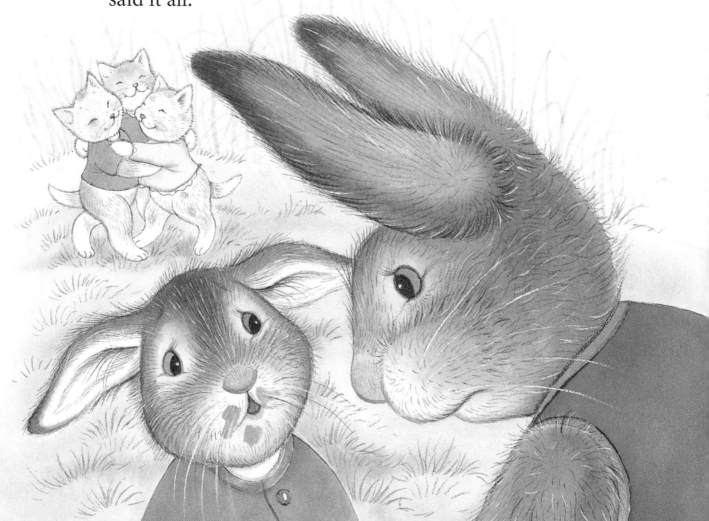

"Come with me," Sir Byron said.

Hopper followed him to the burrow, and the kittens tagged along behind. Sir Byron gave the kittens what was left of Hopper's goodies and made them honorary Easter bunnies.

"Go now," Sir Byron told the kittens. "Spread joy and love!"

The Great Hare turned to Hopper. "As for you," he said, "you shall watch the kittens hide your treats. Perhaps then you'll understand what it means to be an Easter bunny."

It took a while for the kittens to get the knack of hippety-hopping. But they had no trouble at all spreading joy.

Hopper followed as they crossed the forest, hiding a brightly colored egg here, a chocolate bunny there. He watched as young gophers, squirrels, moles, and mice squeaked with delight as they found their treats.

Hopper looked up and saw the clouds change from pink to fluffy white. He saw the first crocuses open their petals.

Hopper felt a lump in his throat. He'd always just worked his route, then gone home to soak his sore paws. He had never noticed the wonder and magic of Easter before. It made him feel happy inside.

Just then Sir Byron appeared at his side. "What do you think about Easter now, Hopper?"

"It's wonderful!" Hopper said.

From then on, Hopper was glad to be an Easter bunny. He didn't mind spending every day of the year making treats for others to enjoy.

And the next year, for the first time in his life, Hopper was eager for the night before Easter.

Finally the magic night arrived. Hopper's feet felt as light as marshmallow chicks as he danced the Easter bunny dance. He couldn't wait to get his wheelbarrow heaped with treats and hide them all over the woods for happy youngsters to find.

When Sir Byron gave Hopper his wheelbarrow, he said, "Since you have an awfully big route for one little bunny, I've arranged for you to have some helpers."

Hopper laughed as the three little kittens popped out from behind the Great Hare.

And as they pushed their delicious load through the moonlit forest with a *hippety, hoppety, mew, mew, mew,* Hopper realized just how much happiness Easter brings.